SUPER SHORTS

Seriously Spooky Stories

KINGFISHER
a Houghton Mifflin Company imprint
222 Berkeley Street
Boston, Massachusetts 02116
www.houghtonmifflinbooks.com

First published in 2007
2 4 6 8 10 9 7 5 3 1

LIBRARY OF CONGRESS CATALOGING–IN–PUBLICATION DATA
has been applied for.

ISBN 978-0-7534-6074-0

Printed in China
1TR/0507/PROSP/MAR/80NEWSP/C

SUPER SHORTS

Seriously Spooky Stories

compiled by Chris Powling

KINGFISHER

BOSTON

Contents

The Bravest Man in the World

Robert Hull

There was once a young man so brave that nothing scared him, not bears, or snakes, or flying arrows, or the shouting of thunder.

Not even ghosts scared him.

Outside the village one night, from down by the river, there was a whistling and hooting like owls.

"Listen," an old man said, "ghost talk.

The ghosts are talking about death and ghastly things, telling ghost stories." His words sent a chill down the spines of the people listening around the fire, but the young man felt only curious to see these ghosts.

He slipped away into the shadows and went toward the river, hoping to find some skeletons sprawled under a tree, chatting in that whistling way that he'd just heard.

He didn't see any ghosts, because the three who were there saw him first. They were having their evening meal: the smells of chicken and fish that drifted from the village. Ghosts don't eat; all they need to keep them alive is the aroma of food.

So when they looked along the path and saw a young man creeping toward them, they slid off in their canoes, gliding through the water quicker than otters; ghost canoes have holes in them and go faster than the canoes of people. Even the brave young man might have shuddered if he'd seen three misty skeletons speeding along in holey canoes and if he'd heard the clunky rustling sounds of paddling bones.

After a while the three

ghosts stopped and pulled their canoes up the riverbank.

"You know," one of them said, "I think I'll go and scare that young man for spoiling our meal. I'll jump out at him on the path and dance around him rattling my teeth."

"I'd like to do that too," said the second ghost.

"I'll go," said the third ghost. "I'm the biggest, so I'll give him the biggest fright. I'll scare him silly."

"It's not how big you are," said the first ghost. "It's how scary you are."

"I suggest a wager," said the third. "Whoever scares that young man the most wins the others' canoes."

"How about a bigger bet? How about our horses?"

"Horses it is."

So it was arranged. The next night the first ghost paddled up to the village to give the young man the scare of his life. He walked along the path—pedaling along in the air a foot or two above the ground, the way that ghosts do—to the edge of the forest, where the path from the village reached the trees. He sat on a branch and started whistling a

well-known tune, swinging his legs
in time to the rhythm.

In no time at all the young man, as
curious as the night before, came
creeping across from the village,
peering into the trees.

The ghost continued whistling till
the young man saw him and stopped.
Then—GOOOOR, GRAAAR,
RRAAAAHHR! The ghost swung
out of the tree with
a howl, rattling his
teeth and whirling his
crackling arms around
as fast as he
could. Then he

started frolicking around and making hooting noises.

The ghost waited for the young man to turn and run. But the young man only listened and looked for a moment and then jumped forward and grabbed an arm bone with one hand and an anklebone with the other. The ghost's hooting turned to a howl as the young man bent his skeleton around into a hoop and tied it up with some grass. Then he started rolling his hoop along the path. The ghost moaned and whined with every clunky turn of the bones. "Don't, don't!" he yelled.

They came to the river. The skeleton trundled along the path and splashed over the edge.

"You look as if you need a good bath, ghost! Your ghost-wife will appreciate it!" And the young man laughed.

Ghosts can't drown, of course, but this one thrashed around in the moonlit river as if he thought he could. To the young man, it was a pretty sight, this ghost taking a bath of glitter. After beating back and forth like a trapped salmon for a minute or two, the ghost finally snapped the grass knot. He staggered back upright

and clunked out, dripping like a fish
basket.

When the other ghosts heard what
had happened, they rattled and shook
with laughter so much that they had
the kind of accident that sometimes
happens to ghosts. They laughed their

heads off. Two skulls rolled down the bank and into the river. Two piles of bones skittered after them into the water, feeling around on the sandy bottom till each found a wet skull and crammed it back on. At first the big skeleton had the little one's skull on, which slipped off; the smaller skeleton went tottering around wearing the tall ghost's skull. It took a minute or two till they got sorted out with the right heads.

The next night the second ghost went to the village. When the young man came along, the ghost jumped out of hiding and threw an arm

around his neck,
hissing, "Dance
with a ghost!
Swing along
with a skeleton!"
"I think I'd like
that!" the young man calmly
said, putting his arms around the
ghost. The ghost couldn't believe
his ear sockets. He couldn't break free
either. The young man's hands had
a tight grip on the dry bones of his
partner's as they started swaying
from side to side. "I'm dancing
with a ghost," the young man sang.
"My partner's a skeleton. But

what should we do for music and rhythm? I know—your little echoey skull."

And as calmly as if he was taking a coat off a hook, the young man lifted the skull off the neck and put it under his arm. Then, pulling a leg bone out from under one of the knees, he began to hammer out a catchy rhythm on the skull. "Dance with me, you dumb skull, you ghastly, ghostly glum skull. Let me thump your drum skull, your empty little numb skull! What a haunting rhythm I'm beating on where your brain was!"

The ghost groaned. "Don't, don't,

my head hurts!"

"You don't have a head, former person full of bones, only a hollow skull. It can't hurt. Ghosts can't feel pain."

"This ghost can. And don't whirl the rest of me around. Don't dance me so hard. I've got dizziness in every bone!"

The young man was whirling the ghost around so fast that pieces started to fly off. A finger bone flipped through the air. An ankle slid off into the bushes. Faster and faster. One, two ribs jangled down into the dust. The ghost was in pieces. The young man laughed, watching the ghost shambling and shuffling around trying to reassemble himself.

The ghost howled. "I will tell my ghost-husband about your cruelty, and he will come and scare you out of your wits."

So it was a ghost-woman that he had danced with! "Even better! I've danced with a ghost-woman!" the young man cried as the ghost-woman limped off down the path, a bone or two still missing.

When the ghost told her story, only one ghost laughed—the third one. He knew how much he was going to terrify the young man and then win the bet. The next night he rode off on his large skeleton horse to find the young man.

The young man was already on the path, waiting. "My horse and I have come to kill you," said the ghost in his deepest, hollowest voice, making his skeleton horse rear up over the young man.

"You cannot kill me," the young man said. "I'm a ghost in disguise— a witch ghost with false eyes, false flesh, and false teeth. I'm an illusion. I can scare you to pieces." And the young man moaned and howled like a pack of wolves—HAROO! HAROOZLE! FAROOZLE! He crossed his eyes and gnashed his teeth. He made piercing whistling sounds. It would have sent a herd of buffalo thundering off in terror. The ghost started to moan and shake, limbs going every way at once, like pieces of scribble. Then the horse under him began trembling too, and after a few moments of terrible shuddering, with the ribs of the horse banging like a gate, the ghost rider toppled off with a clatter. Ghosts can't be knocked unconscious, but this one decided to rest for a while and just sat there.

The young man was delighted. "A horse! I have a ghost-horse! Goodbye, ghost!" And taking the skeleton horse by the bridle, he leaped on its back and rode off down the path.

It was early morning in the village when some women carrying water saw a man on a ghost-horse ride out of the mist. They screamed and ran,

waking everyone around them.
People came peering dozily out of
their tepees, wondering what was
going on. In the dawn mist they saw
a ghost-horse
with a young
man on it. *A
dream left in our
heads from the
night*, each one
thought. They stood
rubbing their eyes, waiting
for the dream to fade. But it didn't.
The ghost-horse with its living rider
came walking slowly through the
village, the young man looking

around him with a big grin on his face, his skeleton horse creaking under him from the unusual load. Everyone gaped as the young man dismounted in front of his own tepee.

An old man went over—the one who had heard the ghosts talking a few nights before. He wanted to touch it, to see if it really was a ghost-horse. He patted the horse on the rump bone. It rattled. He nodded his head as if he understood something. A few other brave people came across and stood around. Soon the young man was telling his story, and soon people were believing him.

That night, around a great fire, the young man told all of the people how he had sent three ghosts to flight and stolen a ghost-horse. When he had told it all once, they asked him to tell it again.

"He is a very brave young man," people said to each other.

"He must be the bravest young man in the world."

"There has never been anyone so brave."

"No one will ever be able to do a braver thing than he has done."

They nodded their heads solemnly.

There were some children sitting around the fire too. After the first hour of listening, they began to get bored. A little girl, who happened to be sitting next to the young man, began playing with a piece of wood at the edge of the fire. She didn't notice when a small wood spider dropped off and ran toward the young man's foot. It ran up over his moccasin, then turned around to go down again, and then decided to try farther up.

The young man felt a little tickle around his ankle. He looked down. A spider!

He screamed and put his arms over his head. "Aaaaargh! Get it off me! Get it off me!" The little girl picked up the spider and put it on her hand, watching it delightedly as it scampered across her palm.

"Look! Isn't it pretty?" she said, holding it out for him to admire.

"Take it away! Take it away!" shrieked the bravest man in the world.

Things That Go Bump in the Day

Tony Ross

Foggy was a little ghost who lived with his mom and dad at the top of a spooky old house.

Foggy was only born around 500 years ago, so he was a very young ghost. He had lived in a lot of places, including a castle, but this was the best. Ghost families like spooky old places because they make them feel

safe. This one had lots of bats and
spiders for pets. There were pill bugs,
too, but they make rotten pets. You
can't teach them anything, and they
are not very playful.

Foggy almost
taught a pill bug
to sit up and beg,
but it kept falling
on its back and
kicking its legs up
in the air.

Foggy loved being a ghost. But
sometimes life got a little BORING.
There are not many things that a
ghost can do. Then Foggy found a

book of ghost stories, and things
began to get better. The first story was
about a ghost who walked through
walls. "That'll be a COOL thing to
do!" said Foggy to a creepy slug. And
he walked BONK into a wall. All he
did, though, was bump his nose.

"Shouldn't believe everything you
read," the creepy slug said, giggling.

The next story was about a ghost
who walked all over a house shouting
"OOOOOHHH!" and waving his
hands in the air and jumping out of
dark places. Foggy thought that was a
silly way to behave, but he couldn't
get the story out of his mind. There

was a whole house beyond the dusty
rooms where Foggy lived. Maybe
wandering around the house going
"OOOOOHHH!" would be less
boring than teaching pill bugs
to sit up and beg.

That morning,
when it was time
to go to sleep,
Foggy's mom gave
him a cobweb sandwich and a glass of
slime. Then she tucked him into bed.

"Mom," said Foggy, "what's it like
in the rest of the house? Are there
any dark places?"

Mom kissed Foggy on the bump at

the end of his nose.

"Don't you dare go into the rest of the house," she warned. "The rest of the house is a TERRIBLE place. Your dad went there once, and he said that it was really scary. He said that it was horribly CLEAN and smelled like SOAP, with sunlight all over the place and lots of knobs on everything. UGH!" she said, shuddering.

Foggy curled up and pretended to go to sleep. The rest of the house sounded exciting, just like an adventure in a book.

When he was sure that his mom and dad were asleep, Foggy got up. He went to the door, and, making himself very small, he slithered through the keyhole and into the rest of the house.

Foggy floated at the top of some stairs. It was true what Mom had said. The house was horribly light, with a funny smell. "That must be soap," Foggy said with a shiver.

Slowly, he went down the stairs. He hovered in the air a little, because there was ticklish, furry stuff spread out all over the floor. He looked around for a friendly bat, even a pill bug, but there weren't any. "Even the creepies don't dare come to this awful place," he said to himself.

With bated breath, the little ghost
floated along the landing. His heart
pounded inside him, and he was
MUCH too frightened to go
"OOOOOHHH!" Foggy wasn't an
especially brave ghost, and by now he
was getting really scared. The rest of
the house wasn't a nice place.

Foggy turned to go back the way that he'd come. Then he saw it! If he'd had skin, he'd have jumped right out of it. It was HORRIBLE.

It was very big, and it was blundering along clutching a small model of itself. It had blue eyes, with hairs all around them, and matted yellow hair hung in twists down its back. Worst of all, when it opened its mouth to snarl, it showed fearsome white fangs. And it smelled like SOAP.

Foggy reeled. Back along the landing he fled, waving his arms up in the air and shouting "OOOOOHHH!" up the stairs,

through the keyhole, to where his
mom and dad sat up in bed,
awakened by all of the commotion.

"Mom," shouted Foggy, "I'VE
JUST SEEN A LITTLE GIRL!"

"Don't be silly," said Mom, hugging
her son. "There's no such thing as
little girls."

A Face in the Dark

Ruskin Bond

Mr. Oliver, an Anglo-Indian teacher,
was returning to his school late one
night on the outskirts of the hill
station of Simla in northern India.
From before the author Rudyard
Kipling's time, the school had been
run along English private school lines;
the boys, most of them from wealthy
Indian families, wore blazers, caps, and

ties. *Life* magazine, in a feature on India, had once called it the "Eton of the East." Mr. Oliver had been teaching at the school for several years.

The Simla bazaar, with its theaters and restaurants, was around three miles from the school; Mr. Oliver, a bachelor, usually strolled into town in the evening, returning after

dark, when he would take a shortcut through the pine forest.

When there was a strong wind, the pine trees made sad, eerie sounds that kept most people on the main road. But Mr. Oliver was not a nervous or imaginative man. He carried a flashlight, and its pale gleam—the batteries were running low—moved fitfully over the narrow forest path. When its flickering light fell on the figure of a boy who was sitting alone on a rock, Mr. Oliver stopped.

Boys were not supposed to be out of school after seven P.M.; it was now well past nine.

"What are you doing out here, boy?" asked Mr. Oliver sharply, moving closer so that he could recognize the rule breaker. But even as he approached the boy, Mr. Oliver sensed that something was wrong. The boy appeared to be crying. His head hung down, he held his face in his hands, and his body shook convulsively. It was a strange, soundless weeping, and Mr. Oliver felt distinctly uneasy.

"Well, what's the matter?" he asked,

A Face in the Dark

his anger giving way to concern. "What are you crying for?" The boy would not answer or look up. His body continued to be wracked with silent sobbing. "Come on, boy, you shouldn't be out here at this hour. Tell me your trouble. Look up!" The boy looked up. He took his hands from his face and looked up at his teacher. The light from Mr. Oliver's flashlight fell on the boy's face—if you could call it a face.

It had no eyes, ears, nose, or mouth. It was just a round, smooth head— with a school cap on top of it! And that's where the story should end. But

for Mr. Oliver it did not
end here.

The flashlight fell from
his trembling hand. He
turned and scrambled
down the path,
running blindly
through the trees and
calling for help. He
was still running
toward the school buildings when he
saw a lantern swinging in the middle
of the path. Mr. Oliver stumbled up
to the watchman, gasping for breath.

"What is it, sahib?" asked the
watchman. "Has there been an

accident? Why are you running?"

"I saw something—something horrible—a boy weeping in the forest—and he had no face!"

"No face, sahib?"

"No eyes, nose, mouth—nothing!"

"Do you mean it was like this, sahib?" asked the watchman, and he raised the lantern to his own face.

The watchman had no eyes, no ears, no features at all—not even an eyebrow! And that's when the wind blew out the lantern, and Mr. Oliver had a heart attack.

The Oddment

Chris Powling

At first, I wasn't afraid of the Oddment at all. I loved everything about it—its ragged shape, its softness and smell, its colors all faded in the sun.

Where had it come from? Was it cut from an old nightgown of my mother's? Or from one of Grandpa's ancient flannel shirts? "Never mind,"

Mom always said when I asked her. "Just count yourself lucky that you've got it at all."

"I do, Mom," I answered.

And I did, too.

To tell you the truth, I couldn't imagine life without the Oddment. It was my Best Friend and my Favorite Toy and my Big Brother all rolled into one. "Honestly," Mom would say, "sometimes I can't tell where that Oddment ends and you begin!"

I couldn't tell either. That's the way it was, and that's the way it always would be.

"Make up, make up, never, never break up . . ."

And we never would.

Not ever.

Even when I started school, it made no difference. I simply took the Oddment along with me. "No problem," the teacher told my mom. "Cuddlies are welcome here."

"Not a cuddly," I said, frowning.

"Well, a comforter . . ." said the teacher.

"Not a comforter."

"A special thing, maybe?"

"Not a special thing," I insisted, stamping my foot. "It's an Oddment."

"It certainly is," the teacher said with a laugh. "But whatever you call it, I wouldn't dream of telling you to leave it at home."

So all through elementary school, the Oddment and I were closer than ever.

Don't ask me why things began to

change when I started middle school. At first, I suppose, I simply forgot the Oddment—and rushed back up to my bedroom at the end of the day to cover it with kisses. Then, every so often, I decided that it was too much trouble to look after it amid all the hustle and bustle of the classroom. "It'll get lost," I complained. "I won't know where to find it."

"Fine," said Mom. "It's your choice."

And she winked at Grandpa, as if she'd expected something like this now that I was older.

Of course, this got me so ashamed that for a while I made more of a fuss about the Oddment than ever.

But only for a while.

Soon I was "forgetting" it regularly.
Even worse, when other kids came to
play, I was careful to tuck it under my
pillow, out of sight.
Once, just to show
who was the boss, I
left it in the bathroom
overnight—a wet,
thunderous night
when normally I'd
have lain in bed
sucking on one corner of it so that I
wouldn't feel frightened. I slept
surprisingly well . . . till I woke up at

daybreak and found the Oddment wrapped around my neck like a scarf and one corner of it actually in my mouth waiting to be sucked.

No, Mom or Grandpa hadn't put it there. I could tell that from how nice they were about it—as if they would have brought it to me from the bathroom if only they'd noticed. "You don't have to grow up all at once," said Grandpa with a grin. "Bit by bit is fine with us."

"Probably you got it yourself," Mom agreed. "But you were too sleepy to remember."

"Or you were sleepwalking,"

Grandpa added.

Mom scolded him about that, in case he'd scared me.

But it wasn't Grandpa who scared me. I knew exactly who'd done the walking while I was asleep.

After that, I admit, I tested out the Oddment. Every evening I stuffed it underneath the sofa downstairs, or clipped it to the clothesline on the patio, or locked it in the shed at the bottom of the yard. But the instant that I opened my eyes the next morning, it was snuggled up beside me in bed.

It had other tricks too. One of them

was hiding in my lunch box so that it was the first thing I saw when I lifted the lid in the school cafeteria. Another trick was wrapping itself around my gym stuff—or tucking itself so carefully in the back pocket of my jeans that I had no idea that it was there, flapping behind me like a tail, till the other kids pointed it out. "Don't worry," they always said. "We've got cuddlies too!"

"You do?"

"Of course we do!"

And they meant it, I'm sure.

By now, though, I was pretty certain that their cuddlies were nothing like mine. My cuddly, my comforter, my special thing was a complete freak. What I'd gotten, really, was an Oddment. And I was beginning to wonder if I'd ever be free of it.

So I decided that it must have an accident—an accident-on-purpose, you understand. After all, nothing could actually hurt an Oddment. A fire would simply burn it up, I guessed, or a toilet would just flush it away under the house. . . .

Probably you can guess what happened. Or *didn't* happen, I mean. After this, whenever my eyes fluttered open in the morning, I found myself sucking on something that was thin and frayed, with a scorched, smoky taste to it and a faint smell of . . . well, the toilet.

No, don't laugh.

I didn't laugh, I promise you—

especially now
that the
Oddment was so
shriveled and so
grisly-looking
that it reminded me
of a stringy piece of
meat, the kind that you can't swallow
however much you chew. It didn't
feel like a scarf around my neck
anymore either . . . more like a strip
of burlap or an old, old bandage.

By now I was desperate—I
don't mind telling you. What really
scared me was the thought that the
Oddment might figure out what was

going on—not carelessness on my part at all, but a plot to destroy it altogether. What would it do then?

Knowing that Mom and Grandpa wouldn't believe me however hard I tried to convince them, I told my teacher instead. Not straight out, naturally, in case she thought that I'd gone crazy too. Instead, I wrote her a story about an indestructible cuddly called a Whatsit—the best story I've ever written. And there, in her comments at the bottom of the page, she gave me the answer to my problem: "This is fantastic—even from a great storyteller like you. It's so spooky that it gave me nightmares last night! Why didn't you finish it, though? Couldn't the Whatsit have been mailed to the other side of the world, for example—so far away that it could never have hoped to get back? It isn't really fair to keep your reader guessing . . ."

Thanks, teacher.

I couldn't wait to get home that day.

Take my word for it—the package that I put together was safe. Outside it looked like an ordinary padded envelope, but inside was heavy-duty plastic surrounding an old metal pencil box of Grandpa's that I'd

wrapped up tight
with industrial-
strength tape. A
rattlesnake couldn't
have broken out
of that bundle,
never mind the
Oddment.

Then came the real
craftiness. The address I wrote on the
label was to a town deep in the
outback of Australia. And it was almost
correct . . . except for the person's
name and house number and street.
These I completely made up.

Finally—a stroke of genius—I gave

the package to an uncle of mine to mail for me in Canada. "My friend wants a Canadian postmark for his collection," I explained.

Now, there was no chance at all that the package would be tracked back to me. It would be stored away forever in some isolated post office down under. . . .

That was three years ago. In all the time since, Mom and Grandpa have only mentioned the Oddment twice. The first was one Christmas when we had a really good laugh about it. The second was last month, on my birthday, after Grandpa gave me his present—a yappy, roly-poly puppy named Spike. "Here you are, already eleven years old," he declared, "and you've never had a pet of your own before—not counting that old rag you used to lug around with you, anyway. What was its name?"

"The Oddment," I said. "Spike will be much more fun than that, Grandpa!"

He certainly is. For instance, I get a present each day now. Usually it's a dog

biscuit or a mouthful of newspaper or a place mat stolen from the kitchen. Whatever it is, Spike lays it on my bed as if it is some kind of treasure and then wags his tail frantically to persuade me that I should take him for a walk as a reward.

Today, though, after breakfast, he brought in something really weird from the backyard. It was twisted and crusty and somehow travel-weary, like a piece of rigging from an old-fashioned sailing ship. But worst of all was its color, which reminded me of the sort of bruise that Mom calls "angry."

Of course, I recognized it at once, and my heart almost stopped midbeat.

There it is behind me, coiled up on my pillow, as I type all of this on my computer. I've been here at the keyboard all day, to be honest. The trouble is, although I think that my teacher is completely right about how unfair it is to leave the reader guessing, I don't have any more idea about the ending of my story than I did the first time I wrote it. And already it's getting close to bedtime.

Tsipporah

Adèle Geras

Here is something that I've noticed:
as soon as candles are lit, as soon as
night falls, my grandmother, my
parents, and all of my uncles and
aunts start telling stories, and the
stories are often frightening, meant to
send small shivers up and down every
bit of you. When the grownups talk, I
listen. I never tell them my

frightening story, even though it
is true. They wouldn't believe me.

A few weeks after my eighth birthday,
my grandmother took me to visit her
friend Naomi. Why, I wanted to know,
had I not met this friend before?

"I never take very young children
to see her. She might frighten them.
The way she looks, I mean," said my
grandmother.

I imagined a witch, a giantess, or
some monster that I couldn't quite
describe. I said, "What's the matter
with her?"

"Nothing's the matter with her.
She's very old, that's all."

I laughed. "But you're very old, and I'm not scared of you."

My grandmother said, "Compared to Naomi, I'm a rosebud, I promise you. Wait and see."

She was exactly right. Naomi was ancient. Her head was like a walnut or a prune, maybe, with eyes and a mouth set into it. She wore a headscarf, and I was glad about that. I was sure that she was bald underneath it. She sat in a chair pulled up to a table, drinking black coffee and smoking horrible-smelling cigarettes. She spoke in a voice like machinery that needed to be oiled. After I was introduced to her, I was supposed to sit quietly while the ladies chatted. I couldn't think of anything worse, so I said to my grandmother, "May I go out into the courtyard for a while? I'll just look at things. I promise not to leave the house."

My grandmother agreed, and I stepped out of Naomi's dark dining room into the sunshine. The rooms that Naomi lived in could have been called an apartment, I suppose, but it wasn't an apartment in a modern building. It was in a part of Jerusalem where the houses were built around a central courtyard, and four or five families shared the building. In this courtyard there were pots filled with geraniums outside one door and some watermelon seeds drying on a brass tray outside another. A small sand-colored cat with limp white paws was sleeping in a patch of shade. Naomi's rooms were on the upper

story of the house. It was around three o'clock in the afternoon. All of the shutters were closed. Maybe everyone who lived there was old and taking an afternoon nap. The sun pressed down on the butter-yellow flagstones of the courtyard, and the walls glistened in the heat. Suddenly I heard a noise in the middle of all the silence: a cooing, a whirring of small wings. I turned around to look, and there, almost within reach of my hand, was a white dove sitting on the balcony railing.

"How lovely!" I said to it. "You're such a pretty bird! Where have you come from?"

The bird cocked its head and looked exactly as though it was about to answer, and then it changed its mind, and in a blur of white feathers, it flew off the railing and was gone. I leaned over to look for it in the courtyard and thought that I saw it, just there, on a step. I ran down the stairs after it, but it was nowhere to be seen.

A girl of around my age was standing beside a pot of geraniums.

Where had she come from? She wore a white dress that fell almost to her ankles. I thought, *She must be very religious.* I knew that very devout Jews wore old-fashioned clothes.

"Have you seen a white dove?" I asked her. "It was up there a moment ago."

The girl smiled. She said, "Sometimes I dream that I'm a dove. Do you believe in dreams? I do. My name is Tsipporah, which means 'bird,' so of course I feel exactly like a bird sometimes. What do you feel like?"

I didn't know what to say. I was thinking, *This girl is crazy.* My name is Rachel, which means "ewe lamb," but I never feel woolly or frisky. My cousin is named Arieh, which means

Tsipporah

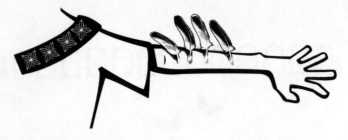

"lion," and he's not at all tawny or fierce. I said, "I just feel like myself."

"Then you're lucky," said Tsipporah. "Sometimes I think I will turn into a bird at any moment. In fact, look, it's happening . . . feathers . . . white feathers on my arms . . ."

I did look. She held out her arms and cocked her head, and I blinked in the sunlight, which all at once was shining straight into my eyes and dazzling me. But in the light I could see . . . I think I saw, though it's hard to remember exactly, a flapping, a vibration of wings, and the *krr-krr* of soft dove sounds filling every space in my head. I closed my eyes and opened them again slowly. Tsipporah had disappeared. I could see a white bird over on the other side of the courtyard, and I ran toward it, calling, "Tsipporah, if it's you, come back . . . come back and tell me!"

The dove launched itself up into the air and flew up and up and over the roof and away, and I followed it with my eyes until the speck that it was had vanished into the wide, pale sky. I felt weak, dizzy with heat. I climbed slowly back to Naomi's rooms, thinking, *Tsipporah must have hidden from me. She must be a child who lives in the building and likes playing tricks.*

On the way home, my grandmother started telling me one of her stories. Sometimes I don't listen as well as I should when she starts on a tale of how this person is related to that one, but she was talking about Naomi when she was young, and that was so hard to imagine that I was fascinated.

"Of course," my grandmother said, "she was never quite the same after

Tsipporah died."

"Who," I asked, suddenly cold in the sunlight, "is Tsipporah?"

"Naomi's twin sister. She died of diphtheria when they were eight. A terrible tragedy. But Tsipporah was strange."

"How strange?"

"Naomi told me stories . . . you would hardly believe them if I told you. I know I never did."

"Tell me," I said. "I'll believe them."

"Naomi always said that her sister could turn herself into a bird just by wishing it."

"A white dove," I said. "She turned herself into a white dove and flew away." My grandmother looked at me sharply.

"I've told you this story before, haven't I?"

"Yes," I said, even though, of course, she never had. I didn't tell her that I had seen Tsipporah. I didn't want to frighten her, so I said nothing about it.

Now, every time I see a white dove, I wonder if it's her, Tsipporah, or maybe some other girl who stretched her wings out one day, looking for the sky.

Widdershins

Ann Turnbull

When they were almost there, below
the granite outcrop, Mr. Ashton said that
they would stop and look at the view.

Michael didn't want to stop; he was
eager to go on, to reach the summit.
But the others were tired. Backpacks
came off and hit the ground; sweaters
followed.

"Can we have lunch now?"

Mr. Ashton looked at his watch and agreed. "Let's sit behind those rocks, out of the wind."

Twenty children began with enthusiasm, unpacking backpacks, pulling out sandwiches, candy, drinks, and chips.

"Up there," Mr. Ashton said, pointing to the piled rocks on the summit, "is the Devil's Chair. See, where those rocks make a shape like a throne? They say that if you run around the Chair seven times widdershins, the

Devil himself will appear."

Michael stared.

"What's widdershins?" asked Paul.

"Wiggleshins, widdleshins," Kelly and Zoe said, giggling.

"Widdershins," said Mr. Ashton, "means counterclockwise."

Hands waved in the air, and bodies turned. "That way." "No, that."

"Let's go!" Paul, Craig, and Robert were off, widdershins around the base of the rocks.

"You won't get far," called Mr. Ashton. "It's not as easy as it looks. And be careful climbing around the Chair," he added to the

retreating figures of Tracey and
Lorna.

"What does the Devil look like, Mr.
Ashton?" asked Jane, a little anxiously.

"Horns and a tail," said Zoe with
relish.

"Maybe." Mr. Ashton smiled. "But
they say that he can disguise himself.
Sometimes he appears as a raven, a
black dog, or a toad."

"Ugh!" said Zoe and
Kelly in unison.

The class began
to disperse; some
went to the
edge and began

drawing the view; others were dutifully filling in their question sheets; the more adventurous swarmed up and around the Devil's Chair.

Michael turned widdershins.

Mr. Ashton was right. The going was hard, and it was not obvious where to go. Michael had to keep looking up at the Chair to make sure that it was still on his left; but he couldn't always get close to it, and sometimes the lie of the land took him far away, and he found himself clambering over piled boulders that looked as if they had tumbled down from the summit in a storm. And it was hot—even in the wind, it was hot. Only sometimes, in the lee of a rock, the wind would drop instantly, and then there was a chill, a stillness, and silence. Silence, and then, far away, it seemed, a thin piping of children, like distant birds.

He struggled on. The hardest part was just below the Chair, where the land fell away steeply in a scree. Michael slithered, and once he slid several yards, grabbing at pebbles that rolled under his hands, before he could scramble back to the safety of the big rocks.

But at last he had completed one revolution. He stepped out, dirty and

bruised, and came
upon sunshine,
and voices, and
clipboarded
papers flapping
in the wind, and
litter-conscious Zoe
chasing chip bags.

Michael pushed back the damp hair
from his forehead. *One*, he thought.
Six to go.

"Michael," said Mr. Ashton, "don't
forget that you're supposed to draw
the view. And there's your
questionnaire to fill in."

Michael edged away. "I'm going

around again, Mr. Ashton."

"Well . . . remind the others if you see them."

Halfway around the second time, Michael caught up with Craig, Paul, and Robert, who were resting.

"Given up?" he asked.

They wouldn't admit that. "Going up to the Chair."

They tried to make it sound like a better idea than continuing, but Michael wasn't tempted. Seven times widdershins, and you'd raise the Devil. He had

to test the experiment; he had to see
if it worked. Michael liked
experiments. They were the only
things that he was enthusiastic about
at school.

He went around again. And again. It
was hard. His legs and shoulders ached.
His hands got cut and scraped
scrambling over the rocks. The boys had
left the Devil's Chair, but some girls
were climbing on it, shouting, the wind
slapping their hair across their faces.

Four times. More than halfway. He
could do it. He *had* to do it.

Five times. Michael was exhausted.
It was no easy job, raising the Devil.

He wondered if it had been done before. You'd have to be desperate and believe in it.

I don't believe in it, Michael thought. And yet he needed to be sure. He couldn't let an opportunity like this pass. Test the theory. Go on. Finish.

Six times. Michael lay spread-eagled on the grass, panting. It was hot—so hot. His whole body ached. The sky glared, and the rocks shimmered.

Mr. Ashton called, "Michael! We're packing up in a minute. If you want to draw your view, you'd better be quick."

"Just once—once more, Mr. Ashton!" Michael jumped up and was away before Mr. Ashton could call him back.

But someone ran after him; a hand touched his arm. He turned. Jane.

"Don't go," she said.

Jane was small and quiet. She had never spoken to Michael before.

"Six," said Michael. "One more. I've got to."

Jane gripped his arm. "Please. Stop now."

Michael shook her off. He heard her calling after him as he struck out on the seventh lap.

It seemed quicker, easier than the others. Like the last stretch of a race,

when you know that you've won. He
seemed to glide over the piled
boulders and up and down the crags
and gullies and across the scree, and
suddenly he was back. He felt elated.
He had done it; he had finished.
Seven times widdershins—and
where was the Devil?

Michael sprang down and rolled on
the grass. The other children cheered.
Except Jane. Michael noticed her
looking up at the rocks, scared. But
Mr. Ashton smiled. "Well done,
Michael. Pack up your bags now,
everyone. It's time to go."

They heaved up their backpacks

Widdershins

and removed the last scraps of litter.
As they turned toward the parking
lot, Michael glanced back at the
Devil's Chair. Something up there
moved. Black. A dog. A big black dog
bounded out from between two rocks
and stood and stared at Michael.

Michael's heartbeat quickened. A
raven, a toad, or a black dog.

"Michael!" Mr. Ashton called.

Michael turned. When
he looked back, the dog
had vanished. *Stupid*, he
told himself. Just a dog.
But where had it come
from?

Back at the parking lot, they saw that several more cars had appeared. Michael was reassured. The dog belonged to some visitors; it was a family pet.

They drove back to school, chattering, comparing drawings, sucking on lollipops. Michael boasted about his experiment and showed off his cuts and bruises.

"Didn't see the Devil, though, did we?" said Paul.

"There was a dog—a black dog," protested Michael, and immediately he felt a chill, remembering the way that the dog had appeared as if from nowhere.

"I never saw it," said Paul.

But Jane had. She looked frightened.

When they arrived at school, it was only 2:30. Mr. Ashton said that they could spend the last hour finishing their drawings or writing about the visit.

The children sighed—they were hot and restless, and all they wanted was to go home.

Michael began drawing. He'd looked up at the Devil's Chair so often as he climbed around it that he thought that he could draw it from memory. He quickly drew the shape of the granite throne and the tumbled rocks beneath.

When he looked at his finished picture, he was pleased. It was good. But—what was that? A dark shape half hidden behind one of the boulders? Something hiding. A dog? He hadn't drawn that. Surely he hadn't. He erased it. But then he thought that he saw it again, behind another rock: a muzzle, the tip of an ear. He erased vigorously and drew more rocks to hide it.

Kelly said, "Mr. Ashton, there's a dog on the sports field."

Michael stiffened. But the others,

glad for a diversion, jumped up with a scraping of chairs and jostled at the windows as Mr. Ashton struggled to retain order.

"Sit down, Paul, Craig. Sit down, Zoe. It's just a dog. We've all seen dogs before." He paused by Michael's table. "That's coming along well, Michael."

Michael looked at his picture. What had he drawn? Was that a shadow behind the rocks in the foreground, or . . . ? He scrubbed with the eraser and made a hole.

The class settled down. Quiet returned. Coughs, rustling paper, whispers.

And then a scream from Jane.

"The dog!"

Michael leaped to his feet. Chairs toppled, and voices erupted. The dog—a big black hound—had reared up against the window, staring in. Mr. Ashton banged on the glass and made shooing movements. The dog dropped down, out of sight, and then sprang up again: its claws scraped on the glass, grating and scratching; saliva hung from its jaws.

Michael stood rigid with fear. Some of the children whimpered; others began banging and shooing.

"Sit down, everyone," said Mr. Ashton. "I'll get the custodian." He went out.

When he came back, Zoe said, "It's gone, Mr. Ashton."

"Probably a stray," said Mr. Ashton. It was almost 3:30. "Pack up your things."

Michael looked at his drawing. There were no shadows now, no odd shapes, and yet . . . The picture made him uneasy. He scrunched it up and hurled it at the wastebasket. Mr. Ashton was startled. "Spoiled it," muttered Michael.

All the way home he watched for dogs. There were plenty of them, of course: terriers, German shepherds, collies, a Great Dane, stately on a leash. Once, out of the corner of his eye, he thought that he saw a black dog behind a wall;  then, again, padding alongside a hedge. He ran, banged open the gate of his front yard, and beat on the front door.

"I'm not deaf," his mother said.

He was home, safe. He dumped his bag, got a drink and some chips, and settled in front of the television.

He stayed in all evening. He ate his dinner, scribbled some homework, and then went back to the TV. His favorite shows washed over him, lulling and reassuring. He'd been imagining things. There were often dogs on the school sports field. And the streets were full of black dogs; it was simply that he was noticing them more today. That one behind the hedge, for instance: surely that was Caesar, the Wilsons' Labrador? Stupid. He'd been really stupid.

He felt sleepy. The cuts on his hands stung.

"You all right?" His mother felt his forehead.

"Tired. It was hot on the trip. We

walked miles."

"You'd better have an early night."

Michael thought with unusual longing of his bedroom, with its posters and comic books, his Mickey Mouse alarm clock, and his Batman comforter.

"Okay," he said.

He went slowly upstairs.

"Wash," said his mother. "Don't forget."

Michael washed briefly, leaving grubby prints on the towel. His head ached. He was sleepy, so sleepy.

He stumbled across the landing and pushed open his bedroom door.

Huge, on the bed, lay the black dog. Waiting.

Bush Medicine

Faustin Charles

Milton Codrington was a bachelor.
He lived in a one-room house in St.
Victoria village, Barbados. He was a
poor, simple man who didn't have a
job nor a trade.

One night he had a dream that
would change his whole life. In his
dream, Milton saw an old woman
picking papaw leaves, putting them

into a boiling pot, stirring the brew, and saying, "Boil for a hour, wait till it cool, then drink—good for all kinda sickness."

The dream ended, Milton turned, opened his eyes, sat up in bed, and then he muttered, "Papaw leaf. I never realize ordinary papaw leaf so good for medicine."

So Milton went to a papaw tree in the backyard of his house, picked some leaves, boiled them in a pan for an hour, and then he said, "Now, how I going to know whether this brew work or not? I not sick with nothing."

Just then a neighbor, Ma Gerty, called to him. "Milton, boy, me granddaughter sick bad, bad with the flu, and I don't know what to do!"

Milton poured some of the papaw leaf brew into a cup and gave it to Ma Gerty and said, "It's like bush tea, but don't put no sugar in it; just give it to you granddaughter to drink."

Ma Gerty stared at the dark green liquid, nodded, and said, "Boy, I ain't have much faith in these bush medicine, but I going give this to she, and thank you." And she went and

 gave it to her granddaughter.

Around 15 minutes later, Ma Gerty shouted from her house, "Milton, boy! It work! The girl better. Praise the Lord!" Ma Gerty was laughing and kissing her granddaughter, who was sitting up in bed, smiling.

"Yes, praise the Lord!" Milton said with a grin. "I tell you it woulda make she better!"

Soon Milton was giving the papaw bush medicine to the whole village. Then people started coming to him from all over the island. Whenever anyone became sick, instead of first going to the doctor or to the hospital, they went to Milton for his papaw leaf brew, and they were cured of all of their illnesses. Milton was convinced that the papaw leaf brew was a magic cure, and he told no one about how he came by it. He felt that he was specially chosen by God to have the knowledge about the papaw leaf medicine.

Milton's fame as

the man with the magic cure spread to other islands. He was a vain man, and he loved the respect that he was getting from all quarters. He took no money for his brew. People gave him food and clothes; that was all he would accept.

Ma Gerty always stood on the veranda of her house watching all the goings-on.

One day, when most of the people had gone away from Milton's house, two men from the city of Bridgetown came to see him. One was named Riley, and he owned a dry-goods store, and the other, Franklyn, was a pharmacist.

"Now, what can I do for all you?" Milton asked.

"Well, it's like this, Mr. Codrington," answered Riley. "We hear about you bush medicine, and we was wondering if you interested in going into business."

"Business like what?" Milton asked.

"What we mean is this," Franklyn said calmly. "You bush medicine is popular all over the islands. Now, suppose you make it and we bottle it and market it and sell it. We can make a lotta money, the three of we together."

Milton looked bewildered.

"You can have big, big house, car and servants, and plenty other nice things," said Franklyn.

"Money mean power, you know," said Riley.

Milton smiled a little. "I always thought that bush medicine is free for all," he said. "After all, bush growing wild all over the place. People pick it and try it; if it work, then they use it and tell others about it. They does never charge money for it."

"I know I was wasting me time coming here, yes," Riley raged. "The man making fun, man. It's people like you who does end up begging by the roadside, and when people check back at you life, they discover that you had a chance of becoming rich, and you didn't take it."

"Riley, man, I tell you don't get on so," Franklyn pleaded.

"How you want me to get on?" Riley snapped. "The man must be crazy, that's all."

"That's not the way to talk to people, man," said Franklyn, who was becoming fed up with the whole idea. "You must control youself."

"All right, all right, man. I sorry," Riley said coolly.

Milton wiped his face with a dingy piece of red cloth and studied the two men carefully. Then he said, "All right, I go do it with all you."

Riley laughed and said, "Now you talking sense, man."

"You see when you give people time to make up they mind, everything does work out all right,"

Franklyn said with smile.

"Now, you must stop giving away the brew free to people, you hear," said Riley. "When they come and ask you for it, you must tell them, 'All freeness done.'"

"All right, then." Milton nodded. "It going to be hard, but I go stop giving it away."

"Mr. Codrington, that'll be in the contract," said Franklyn, still smiling.

Milton felt a very strange feeling welling up in his stomach.

Milton went into business with Riley and Franklyn, and the business prospered. He now lived in a

beautiful house with an
extra-large kitchen
where he boiled the
papaw leaf brew in
large pots on an
electric stove. He

installed a telephone, and when the
brew was ready, he called Riley or
Franklyn, and they sent a van to pick
it up.

They checked it, bottled and
labeled it, and sold it. The profits from
the business were split equally three
ways.

Milton stopped giving the brew
away to people who called at his

home begging for it. He lied and said that he no longer made the brew or that he had forgotten how to make it.

One morning, Ma Gerty called at his home. Milton looked out a window and greeted her sheepishly. "Good morning, Ma. How life treating you these days?"

Ma Gerty was fuming. "Milton, what is this I hearing that you not giving away the bush water to nobody no more. What happening?"

Milton tried to smile, but failed. "Ma, I stop making that. I ain't have no time with it. I doing big business with other things now."

Bush Medicine

"The other day, a woman come to you for some of the bush water, and you tell she, no, you don't make it no more," Ma Gerty said. "That woman did want the medicine for she sick baby, she didn't get it, and now she child dead. You know about that?"

Milton felt sick, and he began to shake all over. "Well, I sorry about that," he said timidly, "but as I say, I ain't making the bush brew no more. It's too much headache and worry, man."

"And what

about them two fellas I see that come to see you some time ago?" Ma Gerty went on. "I know that one of them is a druggist, and the other one own a shop."

"Them is just me longtime friend, man," Milton gasped as his head ached. "I use to know them from me school days, and they did drop in to say howdy, that's all."

"Milton, I feel you up to something. I hope you know what you doing. You suddenly get rich overnight; you think people don't suspect you up to something and something that not nice? You should have a little conscience, man; that woman child spirit going to haunt you."

"I don't know what you talking about, Ma. I does live a good life."

"Boy, you does get me so vex sometimes. All right, when bad luck start blighting you, don't come for my help, you hear!" Ma Gerty glared at him and went off.

And almost at once the bad luck did begin to blight.

As the days passed, Milton started to change. His fingers and arms began to look like the leaves and stems of a papaw tree. His hair grew long and disheveled, and his body resembled the trunk of the tree. On the soles of his feet grew tiny roots. His whole body throbbed with a burning pain, and his skin color changed from dark brown to green. He was ashamed and afraid to go outside his house in the

daytime. He drank large quantities of the papaw leaf brew, hoping to get better and change back to his normal self, but the more he drank, the worse he became.

One night, when Milton was out picking the papaw leaves, he felt a great pain in his stomach, he couldn't move from where he was standing, and suddenly he was a papaw tree.

The spirit of the dead child entered the tree, and it swayed in a gentle breeze.

A Loathly Lady

Susan Price

A long, long time ago and a while
before that, there were three brothers.
And the eldest of these three brothers,
he upped and said to his father, "I'm
off to seek my fortune." And away he
went, riding on a good horse, with a
good greyhound running behind and
a good hawk on his arm. And neither
he, nor his horse, nor his greyhound,

nor his hawk were ever seen again.

Now the second brother saddled his horse, took his hawk on his arm, whistled up his greyhound, and rode off to search for the first brother and maybe to find a fortune of his own. But he never came back either.

Now there was only the youngest brother left, and when he heard nothing from his two brothers, he upped and saddled his horse, took his hawk on his arm, called his greyhound, and rode off to search for them.

He rode by hill, he rode by dale, and everyone he passed he asked for news of his brothers. Yes, they said, two young men had ridden this way before him—and so he kicked his horse and rode all the faster. Soon he was lost in a forest and didn't know how to go forward or back. But then he saw a hut through the trees and thought himself lucky. "Somewhere to shelter for the night," he said to his horse and his hound.

The hut was built of logs and roofed with shingles, but the shutters were hanging off, and worms had gotten into the wood. No one had lived there for many years, and no one was around now. The youngest brother tethered his horse outside the hut, rubbed her down, threw his cloak over her, and left her to graze. Inside the hut, his hawk flew into the rafters to perch, and he built himself a fire and settled down beside it with his hound.

As the hours passed, the dark grew close around the little fire, and the cold drafts grew sharper. The loose shutters banged in the wind, and the trees outside could be heard lashing themselves with their branches. The wind blew in around the broken

 door, making the fire flicker and scattering the old, dried rushes across the floor. And then came a sound like heavy tramping—a thumping of big, heavy feet—coming out of the forest, *tramp*, *thump*, closer and closer to the hut where the man and dog lay huddled together.

Tramp! Thump! Suddenly the doorway was filled with a dark shape. It ducked its head, and into the firelight came a giantess, a hag, a monster—the ugliest old harridan that you ever saw.

A Loathly Lady

How can I tell you about her? Her hair was gray and hung down in greasy strings—so greasy that it seemed like it was soaking wet; and her skin was as greasy and gray as her hair. Her eyes were red with blood, with crusts of yellow matter at the corners, and the lower lids sagged to show wet red linings. And so crossed were her eyes that she could only see the swollen end of her puffy red nose—from which ropes of thick yellow snot hung to her chest. Her lips wouldn't close over her three yellow teeth, and she drooled.

Her spine was curved as much as a

bent bow, and her big-knuckled,
broken-nailed hands hung down by her
bowed knees. The horny yellow nails
on her toes were as hard and sharp as
flint and cut pieces out of the floor as
she crossed it. And the smell of her! The
smell that rolled off her as she came! The
smell would choke a fox; it would curdle
a cesspit; it would make a stone crumble.

This loathly lady came to the
fireside, and she looked at the
youngest brother, and she said, "Food,
give me food."

The reek of her, as she came close,
made even the fire shrink back.
Strings of snot and drool hung from

her face and were tangled in her greasy hair. But her eyes, although they were red and sore, were so sad as she looked at him, as if she knew too well of her own ugliness. The young man was afraid, but he could not bring himself to say anything that would make her eyes sadder. "If I had food, lady," he said, "I would share it with you gladly. But I have no food with me—I had hoped to be out of this forest before night."

The greyhound at his side was curling his lips at the hag and growling. She looked down at it.

"Food," she said.

"My good dog, lady."

"Meat," she said.

And her eyes were so sad, and her ugliness so gaunt, that it hurt the young man to refuse her the only food there was in the hut—yet it hurt him too to think of his good dog, who had loved and trusted him for so long, being gobbled up by that drooling mouth.

"Food," said the loathly lady, and she whimpered. "Food," she said, and tears ran from her sore, sad, blood-red eyes.

"Take him, then," said the young man, and he scrambled up from his place beside the fire and turned his back. Behind him he heard his dog snarl and then shriek; then came a sound of breaking and gobbling, of tearing and gulping. And the young man put his hands to his face to catch the hot tears that spilled for his poor dog—and he could not tell if he did right to feed one poor, hungry creature by ending the life of another.

Then the loathly lady spoke again. "More meat," she said.

The young man turned to find her looking up into

the rafters at his hawk that was perched there. "My pretty hawk—she will only be a mouthful for you."

"More meat," said the loathly lady, and she stared at him through hair and snot and grime with sad, sad red eyes.

With tears running down his own face, the young man raised his arm and whistled, and the hawk flew down to him, fanning his face with air from her wings. She had hardly landed before the lady snatched her away and crammed her whole into her mouth. The young man closed his eyes and turned away, and in a moment the hawk was eaten, bones and feathers and guts and all.

"More meat, more meat," said the loathly lady.

"There is only my poor horse."

"More meat," she said. So the young man went out into the night, untethered his horse, and led her back into the hut. He turned his face to the wall while the lady ate her, skin and bones and hair and guts and all.

And if she asks for more meat, and there is only myself, he thought, *how can I refuse her when I gave her my dog, my hawk, and my horse?*

But the next thing the lady said was, "A bed. A bed." Her tears splashed holes in the dirt floor. "Let me lie down and rest these long, tired bones. Make me a bed."

The young man went out again and used his sword to cut soft green ferns. He carried them back in armfuls and made a deep bed with them, over which he spread his cloak, now that his horse no longer needed it. "Your bed, lady."

She lay down on the bed and sighed, so glad was she to rest at last. "Now come and kiss me," she said.

To kiss that face besmeared with snot and drool, to have his own face

besmeared by the grease of that
rank hair—it made the
young man tremble.
But the sad, sad eyes
stared at him, and he
felt great pity for her. So he
kissed her cheek—and fell senseless,
stunned by her stench.

He woke up when the sun shone in
through the broken shutters and around
the ill-fitting door. When he turned his
head, he saw sleeping beside him the
most beautiful girl that his eyes—or
mine, or yours—had ever seen. Her
hair spread over her shoulders, red-gold
and shining. Her face was smooth and

lovely, and her eyes were a clear blue. She smiled, and she had all of her teeth, and they  were small and white.

She kissed him and said, "You gave me your dog, you gave me your hawk, you gave me your horse. And even more, you made me a bed and covered it with your cloak. But even more, you gave me a kiss, all to please me, as ugly and frightening as I was. And now I give you myself and my land, for I know that your heart is gentle and your eyes see more than what is before them. You will make a fine king."

And he looked around and saw a hut that was no longer a ruin, and it was filled with rich things and comforts. And it would be easy to say that he made a fine king and lived happily ever after with his beautiful queen.

But when he saw her smile, he remembered the hag's teeth crunching on the bones of his good dog, his hawk, and his horse. And whatever had become of his two brothers who had ridden into the forest before him?

The beauty was a hag, and the hag was a beauty, and knowing that doesn't let you sleep peacefully at night.

Mine

Anthony Masters

On the wind, Jo heard someone call
her name. She got off her mountain
bike and listened. For a while she
could hear only a curlew call. The
bracken rustled, the ugly sheets of tin
fencing around the old mine shaft
rattled, and a light plane buzzed like a
mosquito in the Indian-summer sky.
White clouds raced above her, and

the moor smelled sweet.

"Jo."

She started. The call was quite clear now, and there was an urgency to it.

"Jo."

She laid down her bike on the worn track and walked across to the old mine shaft that had been securely closed off years ago— although a couple of the fencing sheets had been wrenched away by the fierce winds that had been raging over the moorland for the last few days. A warning notice lay flat on the rough, clumpy grass a few feet away from the shaft.

DANGER. DO NOT ENTER. DISUSED MINE.

Then the voice came again.

"Who's there?" Jo asked nervously.

There was no reply—only the distant bleating of a sheep and the wailing of the gusty wind amid the tin sheeting.

"Jo." Faintly, she heard the call again.

"Who is it?"

"Come on, Jo!" This time the words were very distinct.

Jo hesitated.

Hadn't she been warned about this old mine? Wasn't everyone supposed to stay clear of it? Suppose someone was in trouble, though, someone she could help? Besides, wasn't there something familiar about the voice?

She walked through the gap.

Below her, the shaft yawned—dim, desolate, and overgrown with brambles. Wooden boarding that had originally covered the abyss hung in rotten shards. Looking down, Jo could only see darkness. Then, as her eyes became accustomed, she could make out gray rock and a ledge that sloped gently upward.

This was the place where they had brought them out, her memory told her. Uncle Jack, Cousin Jem, and her father's friend Billy.

All had been killed in the mining disaster before Jo had been born. She had often ridden up here, curious about the dead men. Of course she'd seen photographs, but what had they really been like?

"Jo. What are you doing, lass? What's keeping you?"

Jo stared down into the void, and the familiar memory stirred in her mind.

"They never found your grandpa, Jo, however much they dug." That's why she came up here, really, to be with the grandfather she had never known.

"Come on, Jo. What's keeping you?"

"But who are you?"

"Some of my friends are trapped. Can you get down?" The voice was urgent now. "I've been trying to find a way out—a way out for all of us. You've got to help me." The urgency increased.

"The way out's up here," said Jo desperately.

"I can't see anything—none of us can."

"I'll get help."

"No time. You coming, Jo?"

An instinct drove her on as she slithered down to the ledge, knowing what she was doing was crazy, but unable to stop herself.

She still couldn't see anything—just a black pit with what looked like sheer sides. She called down into it.

"Hello."

There was no reply.

"Hey!"

Still no reply.

"Where are you?"

The silence was like a wall. Then Jo felt the rock crumbling beneath her feet, breaking up. She pitched into the darkness.

Her shoulder hit something hard, and the painful vibration echoed right through her body. Jo lay there shaking, not daring to move in case she plummeted farther down, closing her eyes against the horror of it all, curling herself up into a womblike shape, cursing her own stupidity. Obviously she had imagined the voice. She must have. Then, in her mounting fear, she hoped that she hadn't, hoped against hope that there was someone there to help her.

Mine

"Where are you?" she whispered and then shouted.

Still no reply.

Jo shifted, reached out a hand, and froze as grim reality swept over her. She was on another ledge—this time narrower—and the void again stretched below in seemingly endless depth. Her shoulder hurt, and she groaned with pain. Then, deep in the shaft below, Jo heard answering groans. So she wasn't alone! Involuntarily, she moved backward—and encountered solid, warm human flesh. Jo screamed again and again. "What's happening? What's happening?"

"You've got to help me, lass."

They were lying side by side—Jo and whoever it was. She could smell sweat mingled with coal dust.

"I got up here—trying to find a way out. The others are down below. Dying, most of them. But some might live—if we can help them." He gasped slightly.

"Are you hurt?"

"Can't breathe—not that well. But I'll be all right."

The groaning below continued, and then someone began to pray in a

Mine

high, keening voice.

"There's a way out," said Jo. "Up there."

"I can't see anything. Must be dust in my eyes."

Jo turned to him at last, summoning up all of her courage, but all she could see was a dark shape, half buried under an overhanging ledge of rock.

"I can see the light," she said. "I think we could climb there." She stared up at the pale sky, which seemed a very long way up above her.

"You'll have to help me."

"Okay." Trembling, Jo clambered to her feet, her shoulder pounding with pain.

"Can you stand?" she asked her companion.

"I don't know."

"Try."

Jo searched for, and found, a gnarled hand. She pulled and felt an answering weight. It dragged at her at first and then seemed not to be there.

"Where are you?"

"Here, lass." A gaunt shape was standing silently beside her, and suddenly Jo felt the deathly chill of the wrist she was holding. She dropped it with a cry, the chill becoming ice, burning into her flesh.

"Can't see anything." The voice was distant now, almost like a sigh in the darkness, and Jo began to shake, the coldness spreading inside her so that she could hardly bear the pain. "Can't see a thing."

"The light's up there."

"I'll take your word for it. Show me where to climb."

"It's steep. I don't know if we'll manage it."

The drifting voice became sharper. "Look lively, lass. There are dying men down there."

"Give me your hand again."

For a moment she felt cobweb fingers. Then they passed through her own.

"Anyone down there?" The voice broke into the emptiness with unexpected harshness.

There was a face above her—a man with a helmet.

"Who are you?" Jo croaked, as if she hadn't spoken for a very long time. She was still shuddering all over, and there was cold sweat on her forehead.

"Police. We were told that the mine was open, so we came up. Then I saw a bike and no one

around. Are you hurt?"

"My shoulder, but it's not too bad. There are other people down here."

"Other people? How many?"

"I don't know. There's been a cave-in."

"What?"

"They're saying prayers. And there's a man beside me."

"Is there?" Her rescuer's voice was reassuring and sympathetic as the

powerful beam of his flashlight swept
over the ledge. "I can't see anyone."

Jo turned quickly back to her
companion. There was no one there,
but she could make out something
lying in the shadows. She leaned
down and picked it up while the
flashlight beam again doused the rock
in brilliant white light. It was a
miner's helmet, dented a little on its
dome just above the light, the way
that it was in the
photograph she
had seen. She
stared at it.

"Hold on,"

said the policeman. "My friend's coming with a rope—and I'm going to lower him down to you. We'll have you up in no time."

"What about the others?"

"We'll get to them," the policeman replied in the same quiet, calm voice.

"Where are you?" called Jo.

There was no reply.

"Who are you?"

Still no reply.

A few seconds later, another policeman came down to her on a rope.

"I'm just going to slip this harness around your waist," he began.

Mine

"Wait."

"No time for that, lass." There was an edge to his voice and a certain unsteadiness. "There could be another rock fall any moment."

"What's that under the rock?"

He swept over the dark cavity with his flashlight. "Could be a skeleton," he said uncertainly. "Yes . . . yes, I think it is. We'll look into that later." The policeman gulped, clearly wanting to get out of there as quickly as possible. "Come on!"

As Jo was swung up in the harness, she cradled the miner's helmet in her arms.

"This was my grandpa's," she said to herself. "And now it's mine."

Acknowledgments